Benny and the NO-GOOD Teacher

by Cheryl Zach
illustrated by Janet Wilson

Bradbury Press • New York

Maxwell Macmillan Canada • Toronto
Maxwell Macmillan International
New York • Oxford • Singapore • Sydney

To a very special (WOW!) group of writers and friends: Judith Enderle, Jill Ross Klevin, Nancy Smiler Levinson, Joanne Rocklin, Herma Silverstein, and Stephanie Gordon Tessler, who helped bring Benny to life

Text copyright ©1992 by Cheryl Zach
Illustrations copyright ©1992 by Janet Wilson

Bradbury Press
Macmillan Publishing Company
866 Third Avenue
New York, NY 10022

Maxwell Macmillan Canada, Inc.
1200 Eglinton Avenue East
Suite 200
Don Mills, Ontario M3C 3N1

Macmillan Publishing Company is part of the Maxwell Communications Group of Companies.

First Edition
Printed and bound in the United States of America
10 9 8 7 6 5 4 3 2 1

The text of this book is set in 14 point Caledonia.
The illustrations are rendered in pencil.

Library of Congress Cataloging-in-Publication Data
Zach, Cheryl.
Benny and the no-good teacher / by Cheryl Zach ; illustrated by Janet Wilson—1st ed.
p.   cm.
Summary: Fourth grade gets off to a bad start for Benny—his friends are in a different class and he has the strict new teacher.
ISBN 0-02-793706-2
[1. Schools—Fiction. 2.Teachers—Fiction 3.Friendship — Fiction.] I.Wilson, Janet, date ill. II. Title.
PZ7.Z165Ben   1992
[Fic]—dc20   91-30588

Contents

1
Bad News

"*I'm ready,*" *Benny said. He closed his new* notebook, the one with the spaceship on the front, and inspected his pencil one more time. Nice and sharp.

"Why are you so excited?" Carlos asked, checking the lock on his bike. "Just because it's the first day of school? It's back to the same old stuff."

"Not this year," Benny told his best friend.

"This year I'm going to be in Ms. Jackson's room. She does really wild things. Last year, her whole class cooked a Chinese dinner, and raised a nest of duck eggs, and made a bug collection. She has two white rats and a parrot and a garter snake in her room—almost a whole zoo. And her class has parties all the time."

"Oh," Carlos said. He sounded envious. "How do you know you'll get Ms. Jackson and not Mr. Evans? He's pretty strict."

"Because I asked her." Benny put his supplies back into his pack. "Last year, I told her I wanted to be in her room, and she said she'd love to have me."

"Gee," Carlos said. "I hope that I get Ms. Jackson, too."

They left their bikes in the bike rack and hurried across the playground. Benny could feel the spring in his step from his brand-new shoes, just like the ones his favorite basketball player wore. He took a little jump as they passed the hoops in the yard, pretending he was star forward for the Lakers.

"Nice shoes," Carlos said.

"You bet," Benny agreed. He looked down at Carlos's new shoes. Nice, but not as nice as his, he decided. Out loud, he added, "I mean, they're okay."

They had reached the fourth-grade wing. Benny knew where to find Ms. Jackson's room. He hurried to the bright red door with the dolphin poster on it, Carlos on his heels. A list of names was posted on the door.

Benny looked down the list.

Annie Abdul-Hai
David Baker
Carlos Delacruz . . .

"Hey, that's me," Carlos whooped. "I made it!"

Benny read the whole list of twenty-seven names, then read it again. His stomach felt hollow. No *Benny Holt*—his name wasn't on the list.

"My name's not here," Benny said. "Something's wrong."

"What are you going to do?" Carlos asked.

Benny looked inside the classroom. Bright posters lined the wall, and on one side he could see a row of animal cages. A girl at a desk in the front of the room waved at him. It was Melissa Wong, who lived next door to Benny.

"Hi, Benny," she called.

Everyone was in Ms. Jackson's room, everyone except Benny.

"I'm going to tell Ms. Jackson she made a mistake and left my name off her list," he told Carlos.

"Hurry," Carlos said. "The bell will ring any minute."

Benny ran across the playground. Ms. Jackson was easy to spot. She had black, crinkly hair and dark brown eyes that smiled even when her mouth didn't. Bright red flowers were splashed across her skirt, and long earrings dangled from her ears. Watching her talk to a woman he didn't know, Benny thought Ms. Jackson looked very pretty.

Benny ran up to her. "Ms. Jackson!"

The two women turned to stare at him. Ms. Jackson's eyebrows arched. Benny realized he had interrupted.

"Sorry," he said. "But this is important. My name's not on your door."

"What?" Ms. Jackson looked surprised.

"Remember?" Benny explained. "Last year, when I said I wanted to be in your room, and you said you'd love to have me?"

Ms. Jackson smiled. "I'd be glad to have you as a student, Benny," she said. "But I can't have *all* the nice people in my room. It wouldn't be fair."

"Oh," Benny said.

"In fact, this year our school has so many fourth graders, we had to add a third teacher at the last minute. I'm sure you'll enjoy being in Mrs. Rumpbill's room."

She nodded toward the other woman.

Benny stared at Mrs. Rumpbill. She was short and rather round, and she wore a plain navy blue dress with brass buttons. She had thick glasses and a long nose. She didn't look like any fun at all.

"Hello, Benny," she said. "My class is in Room Twenty-four, the old tutoring room."

"Oh," Benny mumbled. He walked slowly back across the playground. His new shoes felt as if they'd turned into stone.

Carlos met him at the door. "What happened?" he asked. "What'd she say?"

"I got stuck with a new teacher," Benny told him.

"But I thought you said—"

"Well, I know Ms. Jackson wanted me in her room," Benny said quickly. "But she couldn't take *all* the nice people. It wouldn't be fair."

"I'm sure glad *I* got Ms. Jackson," Carlos

said. "But we won't be in the same room this year." He looked sad.

"I know." Benny felt even sadder.

The warning bell rang shrilly from the school building.

"Guess I'll meet you at recess," Carlos said. He looked happier already. "See you."

Benny frowned. It was all right for Carlos and Melissa and all the other kids in Ms. Jackson's room, but what about him? He was stuck with this new teacher, who looked like a real lemon face.

Benny found Room 24 next door to Ms. Jackson's room. His name was on the list, all right, along with twenty-seven other students'. There was no bright poster on the door, and nothing on the walls inside, either. No animal cages, no reading nook with books all around. No beanbag chairs. A really dull room.

Benny looked at the students milling around the room. He saw Hank "the Tank"

Giwaski, who liked to bend your arm back until he almost broke it, and dorky Derrick Chase. Just great. All the kids he hated would be in this class.

Benny put his backpack on a desk in the middle of the second row. He took out his new notebook and his pencil. His pencil lead had broken. Figured.

Benny walked to the front of the room and stood in line for the pencil sharpener. In front of him, Derrick had a whole bunch of pencils and took a long time. Finally Benny sharpened his pencil and went back to his seat.

A tall girl with curly blond hair sat at his desk.

"You're in my seat," Benny told her.

"Am not," the girl said. "This is my desk. I'm sitting beside Stacey."

Across the aisle, a short girl with straight brown hair nodded. "That's right."

Benny looked around. His backpack and

notebook sat on the last desk at the very back.

"You moved my stuff!" Benny said.

"You can't prove it," the girl said smugly.

Benny thought about pushing her out of his desk. But she was pretty big. Besides, he knew what his parents would say about fighting in school.

He hated sitting in the back of the room. But all the other desks were full.

Mrs. Rumpbill had come into the room. "Everyone take a seat, please," she called.

Benny stomped over to the last desk and sat down. This was going to be one miserable year!

2
More Bad News

*Mrs. Rumpbill checked the roll and col-*lected lunch money. One of the girls giggled, and the teacher frowned at her. Next Mrs. Rumpbill talked about classroom rules; she had a long list. Then she passed out a reading test.

The classroom was very quiet. Through the open windows, Benny heard a big gust of laughter. Ms. Jackson's students were having fun already! He put his head down on his desk and sighed.

After the test, Mrs. Rumpbill listened to all the students read aloud. The tall blond-haired girl's name was Nina Nickelmire. She stumbled a lot when she read. Benny felt glad, until he heard that Nina and Hank and five other students would go to the reading teacher for an hour. Benny and the remaining twenty-one students were stuck with Mrs. Rumpbill.

The class took turns reading their first story, about a boy who learned how to hit a baseball. It made Benny think about recess. Would Carlos remember to wait for him? Or would he lose his best friend forever?

Benny wondered who would be his friend. Definitely not Hank the Tank or dorky Derrick. He looked around the room.

Behind Stacey, a boy in the next row had sandy hair and picked his nose a lot. A boy on the other side had black hair and round glasses. His name was Will. He looked awfully serious, not much like a friend.

Benny thought that recess would never come. When the bell rang at last, he ran for the door.

"Benny!" Mrs. Rumpbill called. "Remember the rules. Don't run in the classroom."

The playground was covered with kids, yelling and laughing and running. Benny looked around, then found Carlos with a group of boys by the basketball hoops.

Carlos tossed a basketball to a tall, dark boy. When Carlos saw Benny, he stopped.

"Hi," he called. "Want to play?"

"He's not in our room," the tall boy objected.

Benny felt weights in his stomach again.

"So what?" Carlos said.

"We don't need any more players on our team," another boy added. "We have enough already."

"It doesn't matter," Benny said. "I didn't want to play, anyhow."

Carlos looked disappointed, but when a fat boy dribbled the ball toward him, he turned away.

"I'll see you later," he called over his shoulder.

"Yeah," Benny said, scuffing his toe on the blacktop. So much for his new shoes. He couldn't even try them out on the basketball court. As he walked away, he heard the thud of the ball hitting the blacktop and the yells of the ballplayers. They were having fun.

He trudged across the playground. All around him groups of kids played four-square or tetherball. Some girls huddled in small groups to talk and giggle and point at the boys.

Benny felt very alone. He walked across to the swing set and sat on one empty swing. He wouldn't even mind seeing Murray, who lived down the street from Benny. But the

fifth graders didn't hang around with fourth graders.

What a rotten year this was going to be.

Then he heard a shrill whistle blast. Benny looked up to see Mrs. Rumpbill waving her hand.

"My class, over here," she called.

Now what?

Benny walked across to the teacher, dragging his feet.

Mrs. Rumpbill lined up her whole class along the edge of the pavement. "We're going to exercise," she told them. "This will help your body grow, along with your mind. First, let's stretch out."

Benny held up his arms as directed, then shrugged his shoulders and rolled his head. This was boring. Benny felt sure that Ms. Jackson's class was having more fun than this.

Next, Mrs. Rumpbill jumped up into the air, jerking her short, stubby arms together.

"Now, all together. Jumping jacks!"

Benny hated jumping jacks. Everyone around him jerked up and down like puppets on strings. Hank the Tank leaned toward the row in front and gave Will a hard push when the teacher wasn't looking. Will staggered, almost falling into Benny. Benny put out one hand to hold him up.

"Benny," Mrs. Rumpbill called. "Pay attention. And keep your hands to yourself."

Benny jumped harder.

Next they did running in place and push-ups and sit-ups.

Benny was glad when the bell rang. As the class walked inside, everyone grumbled.

"We didn't have to do jumping jacks last year," Nina complained. "I wanted to play foursquare."

"Old Broad Rump should do her aerobics by herself," Hank the Tank added. "She's the one who needs to exercise, not us."

Back in Room 24, Benny thought about Carlos. He'd never get to play with his best friend. And his toe hurt. No wonder—his sock was all scrunched up inside his new shoe.

Benny sat down at his desk and bent over to untie his laces. He pulled off his shoe, then his sock, once white and now dusty gray. Benny wiggled his toes, frowning.

"What are you doing?" Nina turned around in her desk to stare at him. "Why is your shoe off?"

"None of your business," Benny told her. What a nosy person. Anyhow, he still felt angry at her for stealing his desk.

"Why not?" she demanded. "Oh, look, Stacey. What a smelly, dirty old sock."

Benny frowned. "It's not old. What's wrong with my sock?" He lifted his sock to sniff. It didn't smell. Well, not much.

Nina pinched her nose together with her fingers, and Stacey giggled. Benny waved the sock in Nina's direction.

"Don't!" Nina shrieked.

"What's going on here?" Mrs. Rumpbill

left her desk and walked to the back of the classroom. She stood between them and frowned.

"He waved his smelly old sock in my face," Nina said, sniffing. "I have a delicate stomach. I think I'm going to throw up."

"Then go to the rest room," Mrs. Rumpbill said quickly.

Nina jumped up. Behind Mrs. Rumpbill's back, she made another face at Benny.

What an airhead, Benny thought.

"Benny, when Nina gets back, I want you to apologize," Mrs. Rumpbill said.

"What for?" Benny felt more and more insulted. It was all Nina's fault, anyhow.

"Now, Benny, we don't want to start fourth grade as a troublemaker, do we?"

Benny didn't know what Mrs. Rumpbill wanted. He wanted out of this stupid class, away from Mrs. Rumpbill, and far, far away from dumb Nina Nickelmire.

"Benny?"

Benny had a great idea!

21

3

Rats

"*Maybe*," *Benny mumbled, still thinking.* Last year, James Macdonald had been transferred out of Ms. Willis's room, because the third-grade teacher found James impossible to deal with. Could Benny be impossible?

"What's that?"

Benny stared at his desk, refusing to meet the teacher's gaze.

From the corner of his eye, he could see that Mrs. Rumpbill shook her head.

"Time for science." She walked back to her desk. "Let's open our books."

Nina took a long time in the rest room. When she finally came back to class, Mrs. Rumpbill stared at Benny until he muttered, "Sorry."

Nina smirked. Stacey giggled.

Benny thought about what he'd say to them if the teacher wasn't there.

At lunchtime, Benny sat all by himself at the end of the table. Well, not exactly alone. Dorky Derrick sat opposite him on the other side, but Benny didn't feel like talking.

"Look out for Benny and his killer socks," Nina called as she and Stacey went by with their trays. She kicked the leg of his chair, accidentally on purpose. Nina the Menace. Benny gave her a dirty look.

Benny took a small bite of his taco, then

put it back on his tray. He didn't feel like eating.

Benny was very glad when the day finally ended. Just before the bell rang, Mrs. Rumpbill announced, "Tomorrow we'll do some creative writing. Your assignment is to imagine that you are a vegetable."

A vegetable? Benny shook his head. How dumb could you get? This teacher was weird.

When class ended, he grabbed his backpack and ran for the door. He wanted to find Carlos. At least they could ride home together.

Outside, Benny looked around for his best friend. The walkway was crowded with boys and girls, tall and short and skinny and wide, but there was no sign of Carlos.

At last Benny put on his helmet, got on his new, blue bike, and headed for home, all by himself. He pedaled slowly to Tulip Street, thinking about his plan. Would it work?

He was happy to see his own neat, cream-colored house in front of him. Benny had never felt so glad to be home. He pushed the front door open and almost fell over a walker.

"Look out," Benny's mom called from the kitchen. "Don't step on Sasha."

The baby girl in the walker grinned at him. She had big, dark eyes, black corkscrew curls, and a wide grin, smeared with wet cookie.

Benny grinned back.

But when she reached for him with cookie-covered hands, he stepped away.

"Hi, Mom," he called.

"How was fourth grade?" Mrs. Holt answered.

Before Benny could answer, he had to dodge Kevin, his own baby brother. Kevin took shaky steps across the living room, trying to hug Benny's knees.

Benny patted the baby on the head. "Not now, kid."

A blond-headed two-year-old came hur-

tling out of the kitchen. He was also smeared with cookie crumbs. "I-ya," he yelled.

"Hi." Benny's stomach rumbled, and he remembered his uneaten lunch. "Can I have a cookie, please?"

Mrs. Holt looked out of the kitchen doorway. " '*May* I have a cookie.' Of course. Oh dear, I think the babies just ate the last one. How about a graham cracker?"

"Never mind," Benny muttered. He headed for his room.

Ever since his mother had started babysitting, she didn't seem to have any time left over for her very own children.

"It means I can earn some money and still stay home until Kevin is older," Mrs. Holt had explained to her family. It didn't sound too bad at first, but now—

Benny reached the small bedroom he shared with baby Kevin. He shut the door so he could be alone and dropped his backpack.

His bed looked rumpled. One of those "sitter" kids had been napping on *his* bed, Benny thought darkly. Three of his books had been knocked from the shelf—one dog book and two of his best mysteries. He saw a scrap of paper sticking out from under the edge of the blanket. He pulled out the fragment and groaned.

His favorite Superman comic, and someone had ripped the cover! School was awful, and home wasn't much better. What next?

"Mom! Someone's been messing with my stuff!" he yelled from his doorway.

"In a minute, Benny," Mrs. Holt called from the kitchen. "I can't come just now."

His mom didn't even have time for an argument!

Benny stomped into the hall and picked up the phone, glad that his big sister wasn't home yet. Grandpa said Angie always had one ear glued to the telephone.

Benny dialed Carlos's number. His best friend answered.

"Hi," Benny said. "I looked for you after school. What happened?"

"Tim and I stayed late," Carlos said. "We're building a maze for Alexander."

"Who's Tim?" Benny wanted to know.

"One of the guys in my class," Carlos told him.

Benny's stomach knotted again. "So, who's Alexander?"

"One of the white rats," Carlos explained. "The big one with the pink spot on his nose. How'd it go in the new class?"

"Lousy," Benny said. "There's this icky girl named Nina in my room, and she got me in trouble."

"Bad luck," Carlos told him. "We had a good time. I got to hold Alexander during break."

Benny felt worse and worse.

"I've got to go," Carlos said. "Tim's here, and we have work to do."

Benny swallowed hard. "Sure," he said. "Me, too."

Back in his room, Benny opened his backpack and glanced inside. He thought about Mrs. Rumpbill's instructions. Imagine being a vegetable—no way. How could he be a vegetable? Mrs. Rumpbill was too wacky.

Benny pulled his damaged comic book out from under the bed. Superman would know what to do with Mrs. Rumpbill, Benny told himself. He'd probably zap her with his X-ray vision, and she'd never come back to school again.

Benny read his comic and then a chapter in his favorite mystery until his mother called him to dinner. Good smells drifted from the kitchen, and Benny hurried to wash his hands.

He saw that Angie was home from high school, Dad had come in from work, and Grandpa was back from the senior citizens' center. They all gathered around the table.

"How was school, Benny?" his dad asked.

"Awful." Benny helped himself to mashed

31

potatoes, glad to see that the sitter babies had gone home.

"What?" His mom looked up from slicing the chicken. "You didn't tell me that."

"You were busy." Benny chewed glumly on his potatoes. Somehow, dinner didn't taste as good as usual.

"What's so awful?" his mom wanted to know. "I'm not busy now." She handed the platter of chicken around the table and gave Kevin a piece without any bones.

"I'm not in Ms. Jackson's room," Benny told them.

"So?" Angie demanded. "Who said you would be?"

"But I asked for her." Benny tried to explain. "It isn't fair. Carlos and Melissa and all my friends are in her room. I don't have anyone to be friends with."

"That *is* bad," his mother agreed. "Maybe you can make some new friends, Benny."

"Give it your best try," Dad said.

"Might turn out to be better than you think," Grandpa told him.

Benny wasn't so sure.

"How was your first day in high school?" Mom asked Angie.

Angie wrinkled her nose. "Totally decent," she said. "This hunk in my algebra class thought I was a sophomore. Really. Susan and I are sharing a locker, and we have two classes together."

Everyone had friends except Benny. He looked around at his family. Angie was still talking about school. Baby Kevin was smearing his high chair with mashed potatoes. Benny wished he could be a little baby who didn't go to school, or a grown-up high school student like his sister.

Then he remembered his plan. Benny felt better. He'd give it his best try, just like his dad said!

4

Two Good Tries

When his mom called him on Tuesday morning, Benny was dreaming about Nina Nickelmire chasing him with a giant sock. He sat up in bed and yawned. What could he do to keep nasty Nina off his case?

While he dressed, Benny made careful plans for school. He rode to school by himself, without even looking for Carlos at the

34

street corner. After all, Carlos had a new friend to ride with.

Mrs. Rumpbill's room still looked drab and plain. The bulletin boards were still empty. The shelves in the back of the room held only a handful of books. Honestly, Benny thought, this must be the worst room in the whole school, and the worst class, and the worst teacher.

"Just my luck to get a no-good class," Benny grumbled to himself. "With a no-good teacher." But not for long—he had a plan.

"What are you griping about?" Nina turned to stare at him.

"Nothing," Benny told her. "Don't be so nosy."

Nina sniffed. "Nosy, me? I'll show you who's nosy!"

She took a rubber band from her pocket and flipped a paper wad at him. Benny didn't duck in time, and the rolled-up paper stung his cheek.

Enough already! Benny looked around the room; the teacher hadn't come in yet. He felt under his desk. This was war.

"I brought something from home for you," he said.

Nina looked surprised. "You did? What?"

"This." Benny reached into his backpack. He pulled out his favorite squirt bottle, carefully filled with his secret weapon—water colored with grape juice.

He squirted Nina right in the nose.

Nina shrieked. Big purple drops dripped onto her yellow T-shirt and jeans. "Yuck! Look what you did. I hate you!"

Benny laughed. This was more like it. He'd teach Nina not to pick on him.

Nina jumped up and ran toward the door.

She wouldn't get away that easily. Benny ran after her. Just as Nina ducked through the doorway, Benny took aim again. But the purple stream hit someone else instead.

Coming into the room, Ms. Jackson caught

the liquid right in the middle of her chest. The teacher looked at Benny, her brows raised, her dark eyes glittering. "Benny! What on earth?"

Benny stared in horror at the dark stains on her lacy white dress. He had never seen Ms. Jackson angry before. He wished he could disappear.

Behind Ms. Jackson, Mrs. Rumpbill took a deep breath. "Benny!" the teacher echoed.

Benny lowered his squirt bottle, his heart beating fast.

Nina's mouth hung open. Stacey gasped. The whole class sat very still. Everyone stared at Benny and the two teachers.

Ms. Jackson shook her head, her voice icy. "I'll help you with the files later, Agnes, when you have your class under control. Right now, I need to see what I can do to save my new dress." She stalked out of the room.

Mrs. Rumpbill's face had turned very red.

She held out her hand for the squirt bottle. Sadly, Benny handed it over.

Mrs. Rumpbill looked him up and down. "Benny and I are going to have a little talk," she said grimly. "I want the rest of you to work quietly."

Benny followed her out of the classroom, his feet dragging. He hadn't meant to make Ms. Jackson angry, just Mrs. Rumpbill. Now no one would want him.

Outside, Mrs. Rumpbill shut the classroom door behind them.

"All right, Benny," she said. "You must know better than to do something like that. Why did you do it?"

"I didn't mean to hit a teacher," he told her truthfully.

"But you did mean to squirt Nina."

Benny grinned at the memory. Then he looked at Mrs. Rumpbill again, and his grin faded.

"She's picking on me," he muttered. "She

threw something at me first. She's always getting me into trouble."

"If you behave, Benny, no one can get you into trouble. Blaming other people is what babies do."

Benny felt insulted. A baby—him!

"I don't expect any more fighting with Nina," Mrs. Rumpbill told him. "You will apologize to Nina and write a letter of apology to Ms. Jackson. Then this is what you will do. . . ."

Benny knew that it was not going to be a happy day.

He spent both recesses picking up trash from the school grounds. At least he missed the jumping jacks, Benny thought, but the sun was hot and his trash bag got awfully heavy before he was done. He didn't have the chance to see Carlos, but Carlos was probably busy, anyhow.

The only good thing was that Nina didn't speak to him the rest of the day. She didn't even look at him, keeping her back turned all the time. Benny thought it was great.

Before Mrs. Rumpbill was finished with him, Benny had to stay after school for thirty minutes to separate cans and bottles from the garbage for the recycling bins. Then he rode home all alone, and he didn't even get his squirt bottle back.

When Benny got home, his whole house seemed full of crawling, walking, fussing, babbling babies.

He went to his room. One of the sitter babies had wet on Benny's blanket, and his bed smelled.

"Pweey," Benny said in disgust.

"Don't sit on your bed, Benny," his mother called. "I'll put clean linen on it after dinner."

Benny wandered out to look into Grandpa's bedroom behind the garage, but Grandpa wasn't there. The garage was empty, too. Benny sat down on the old brown chair and thought about his day. Maybe his plan to be impossible wasn't so good, after all. But he had to do something to get out of his no-good class!

Benny thought about it for a long time, until the shadows in the garage grew darker. Then he heard a small noise. What was that? Benny listened hard.

"Benny, time to eat," his mom called.

That wasn't it. Benny sat very still, and the noise came again—a faint rustling from the corner.

Benny went to look.

5

Harold

Benny tiptoed across the concrete floor. He heard the tiny noise again. It came from behind the stack of newspapers waiting to be recycled. Benny pushed the stack to one side.

A small, tan body darted across the garage. Was it a mouse? A large, hairy mouse?

"It's a hamster!" Benny yelled. "Almost

like the one Carlos had last year." He ran after it.

The hamster ran up Mr. Holt's workbench, across the top, and down the other side. Benny grabbed a battered bucket from the floor and ran after it. The hamster came to the corner of the garage and stopped, huddling behind an old broom.

Benny watched to see which way it would go. The hamster dashed back toward the workbench. Quicker than thought, Benny scooped it up into the metal bucket.

The hamster scritch-scratched on the side of the pail, trying to climb the slick metal. Finally, it gave up and sat quietly on the bottom.

He'd captured a hamster! Benny grinned, delighted at his speed and good aim. Now what? The hamster needed a better home. But dinner was waiting, and all Benny could find was a cardboard box. He knew that wouldn't work; the hamster would chew a hole through and escape again. The pail would have to do for now.

Benny searched for a plastic top to fit the pail and found one on the shelf beside the workbench. He punched air holes in the top so the animal could breathe. He glanced in to check on it. The hamster sat very still, looking back at Benny with small beady eyes.

"Don't be scared," Benny told it. "I'm not going to hurt you."

Benny ran to the kitchen. "Mom, Mom!" he yelled. "Someone lost a hamster and I caught it. Can I keep it, please?"

Mrs. Holt looked up in surprise. "Maybe you should try to find out where it came from," she suggested.

"I'll ask around the neighborhood," Benny promised. "But can I keep it if we don't find the owner?"

His mother stirred a big kettle of spaghetti sauce on the stove. "I don't know, Benny.

With all the babies in the house, I'm not sure a hamster is such a good idea. I don't want it to get hurt."

Benny frowned. Those dumb sitter babies again, spoiling everything. Then his frown faded. He thought about Carlos and Tim and the maze they were building. Ms. Jackson had white rats in her room.

Maybe Mrs. Rumpbill would like to have a hamster. It wasn't as good as two white rats, but Benny thought that Room 24 needed any help it could get. And maybe he could build a maze, too, and train his hamster just like Carlos and Tim had trained their rat. It would be more than a pet, Benny told himself. It would be a science experiment.

"I'll take it to school," he suggested.

"As long as it's okay with the teacher," his mom agreed. "Dinner's ready; wash your hands."

"Just a minute," Benny told her. He found half a cookie Kevin had left on his high chair and hurried out. Back in the garage, he removed the lid, dropping the bit of cookie into the pail. The hamster quivered.

Benny watched, holding his breath. In a moment he was happy to see the little animal nibble cautiously at the cookie.

"Good," Benny told it. "I'll give you more later."

Benny felt more cheerful. With a hamster in Mrs. Rumpbill's room, maybe his no-good class would be a little more fun.

He walked back to the house, grinning.

"Was school any better today?" Mrs. Holt asked, straining the spaghetti.

"Not really," Benny said. "But I'm working on it."

Wednesday morning, Benny couldn't wait to get to school. He pedaled hard on his bike, the pail with the hamster inside hung carefully over his handlebars. He'd given the animal a good breakfast of cereal and toast, with a tiny jar lid full of water to drink. After he got the hamster to school and showed it to Mrs. Rumpbill, Benny planned to build a proper cage.

He thought he would call the hamster Harold. Benny felt much better. Even if he didn't have any friends, he did have a hamster.

In the classroom, Benny set his pail carefully on top of his desk. He looked around. Mrs. Rumpbill was nowhere to be seen.

Who else would like to see his hamster?

Benny waved at Will. "Want to see something?"

Will shrugged. "What is it?" He stared at the bucket with the lid on top.

In the next row, Derrick looked up. "I want to see, too."

"It's a surprise, and I caught it myself." Benny grinned. "I thought this boring old room needed something fun."

A tiny scratching noise came from the

bucket. Looking curious, the boys came closer.

Behind him, someone poked Benny in the ribs. He looked around.

"What've you got in there?" Nina was back, nosy as ever, with Stacey beside her. Both girls wore pink T-shirts and had their hair pulled into ponytails on the right sides of their heads. Nina's was longer.

"None of your business," Benny said sharply. They thought they were so smart, dressing alike. "Go away. I'm showing Will and Derrick."

"I can see, too," Nina argued. She reached for the bucket.

"Stop!" Benny yelled, trying to push her away.

Too late. In the scuffle, Nina knocked the bucket onto its side, and the plastic lid fell off. A tiny tan streak raced across Benny's desk and down to the floor.

"You let Harold out!" Benny yelled. "Harold, come back."

"Yike—a dirty old mouse," Nina shrieked. She backed away, bumping into Stacey.

"No, it's a hamster," Stacey said. "It's cute. Can I hold it, Benny?"

"Does it bite?" Derrick asked.

Benny didn't have time to answer. He chased the hamster across the room. When the little hamster ran under a whole row of desks, Benny had to duck around them.

Shouting, the other students jumped to their feet. Some of them joined in the chase.

"I've got him!" Will called. He hit the floor with a solid thud, but the hamster dodged the other way. Will looked up, dazed, a few drops of blood dripping from his nose.

"Oh, blood. I'm going to be sick," Nina shrieked. "I have a delicate stomach."

Nobody paid any attention. Benny raced after the hamster.

Harold ran up a bookcase.

"We've got him," Derrick called, panting. "He's behind the books."

"I can reach him," Stacey offered.

"Let me," Benny insisted. "He knows me. I hope."

He put the pail in place and pushed a wooden ruler gently behind the books, hoping to make Harold run into his home.

Suddenly, he felt a sharp jerk and pulled the ruler back. There was a piece bitten out of the end!

Benny shook his head. "I'm not trying to hurt you, Harold," he said, bending over to peer behind the row of books.

Harold didn't seem to understand.

"Try this," Derrick said. He handed Benny a metal rod from the supply closet, and Benny poked behind the books again.

The hamster darted out the other side. Benny and Will and Derrick and Stacey and a whole lot of other kids chased after him. It was like a parade, only faster.

Up the room and down the room they

went, knocking over desks, books and papers flying.

"Catch him," Will called.

"Here—knock him on the head," Nina ordered. She had found a baseball bat in the closet.

"Don't you dare—he's my hamster!" Benny shouted. "You'll flatten him!"

"There he goes," Derrick said.

"Let me," Benny told them, panting hard.

Harold had almost reached the threshold of the open door, with Benny close behind, when Mrs. Rumpbill walked into the room, her arms full of papers.

The little hamster didn't stop; it ran right up Mrs. Rumpbill's leg.

The teacher shrieked and threw her armful of papers into the air. Unable to stop in time, Benny hit the teacher headfirst, knocking her backward. She sat down with a thump, her expression dazed. Benny fell on top of her.

The hamster ran back down her leg and out the door, speeding to freedom.

Sprawled across Mrs. Rumpbill's outstretched legs, Benny felt very sad. "Goodbye, Harold," he called. "I hope you find your way home."

Sneezing, Mrs. Rumpbill began picking up her papers. She glared at Benny.

Definite big-time trouble.

6

Banished

Mrs. Rumpbill talked about thoughtless people. Mrs. Rumpbill talked about having no respect for school property or classroom rules. Mrs. Rumpbill talked about trouble-makers.

Mrs. Rumpbill sure knew a lot of ways to make a guy feel bad, Benny thought.

When Mrs. Rumpbill finally ran out of things to say, she shook her head at Benny.

"You haven't even said you're sorry!"

"I'm very sorry," Benny said. "I lost my hamster."

Mrs. Rumpbill pressed her lips together. "I don't want to see any more of you for the rest of the day."

"I could go to another class," Benny suggested hopefully.

"You'll go to the principal's office, young man, right now. I've got to put my room back together." She went into the classroom and shut the door.

Benny trudged slowly down the walkway, his shoulders sagging. In the office, there were three children ahead of him. One had a headache, one had scraped his knee and needed a bandage, and one had a fever. The school secretary finally got to Benny.

"What are you doing here, Benny? Are you sick, too?"

I wish, Benny thought. He said, "I have to see Ms. Toymoto."

The secretary shook her head. "Not today. A kindergarten student fell off the slide, and Ms. Toymoto and the school nurse have taken her to get stitches and an X ray. You'll have to come back tomorrow; I'm all by myself and very busy right now."

Benny nodded and walked outside. He couldn't go back to class; Mrs. Rumpbill didn't want to see him anymore today. The secretary didn't want him in the office. In fact, nobody wanted Benny.

Benny didn't know what to do. He got his bike, put on his helmet, and rode slowly away from the school building. Maybe he should just go home.

He pedaled two blocks and then stopped on the corner. If he went home now, his mom would want to know what was wrong. Maybe his mom would be angry, too. What would Dad say, and Grandpa? Angie would laugh.

Benny decided not to go home just yet.

He headed for the park instead.

Resting his bike in a shady spot, Benny sat down on the nearest bench. The only people around were babies with their mothers and one gray-haired lady sitting on the next bench, knitting. This was no fun.

Maybe Mrs. Rumpbill was right; maybe he was a troublemaker. It made Benny's stomach feel hollow again just thinking about all the things she had said. He could tell that Mrs. Rumpbill didn't like him.

So much trouble over a hamster. And a *little* hamster, too.

It was the longest, most boring morning Benny could remember. He could go to the park building and ask to check out a basketball, but he was afraid they would ask him why he wasn't in school. Anyhow, shooting baskets by himself wasn't much fun.

He wished he had his new library book to read. He wished he had someone to play ball with. He wished he was in Ms. Jackson's class. Except maybe now she didn't like him, either.

Benny tried to think what to do, but the memory of Mrs. Rumpbill kept getting in the way. Mrs. Rumpbill thought he was bad.

Benny wondered if he had been a troublemaker all the time and just didn't know it. Probably only troublemakers made plans to get transferred out of their classes, even no-good classes. His idea didn't seem so good anymore.

Pretending to be a vegetable might not have been so weird, Benny thought. Maybe he could have been a smelly, grumpy onion or a lean, mean string bean.

Benny watched the little kids on the playground. Two girls slid down the slide, and two boys and a girl built a sand castle.

At the other end of the big sandbox, one little boy sat all by himself, just like Benny. He wore blue overalls and a big frown.

Benny wandered over and sat down on the

corner of the sandbox. "Hi. Why aren't you playing with the other kids? Don't you like building castles?"

The little boy frowned even deeper. "They don't like me."

"Why not?"

"I threw sand in their faces."

"So don't throw sand," Benny told him. "Good grief. Don't you want to have friends? Sitting by yourself is no fun. Give it another shot."

That was what his dad had said. Benny heard his stomach rumble. It must be almost lunchtime at school. Or maybe break. Maybe he should go back.

Maybe not. Probably by now everyone at school had heard about Benny and the hamster. Carlos and all his friends from last year would laugh. They wouldn't like him anymore, either. And all the kids in Mrs. Rumpbill's class knew that Benny was a troublemaker.

Benny shook his head. He had to go back sometime. Maybe he should get it over with, tell Mrs. Rumpbill he was sorry, try to explain about the hamster.

The little boy in the overalls edged closer to the group around the sand castle.

"Good luck," Benny said.

Benny took the lock off his bike, put his helmet back on, and pedaled toward school. When he parked his bike at the bike rack, his knees felt weak. He could hear shouts and laughter coming from the playground.

Benny headed for the basketball court, hoping to find Carlos or Will or even Derrick, who didn't seem like such a dork anymore.

He didn't see Carlos. Benny caught sight of Will, but Will turned away.

Probably didn't want to play with a troublemaker, Benny thought glumly.

Then he heard someone yell.

Benny looked around. He saw Hank the

Tank twisting a smaller boy's arm. It was Derrick, and his face was very pale.

The other boys and girls backed away. Benny took a step backward, too. He didn't want *his* arm twisted.

But then he stopped. Derrick had helped chase his hamster. Derrick was crying.

Benny walked up to Hank. "Stop that," he said.

Looking surprised, Hank stared down his nose at Benny. "Going to tell on me? You'll be sorry. I'll get *you* tomorrow."

"I'm not going to tell," Benny said. "But you have to let him go."

"Who's going to make me?" Hank gave Derrick's arm another hard twist. Derrick groaned.

Hank looked very big and strong. Benny swallowed. "I am," he said, not very loudly.

Hank's grin showed buckteeth. "Get lost. I can trash you with one hand."

Probably, Benny thought. He looked at

Derrick again, then raised his chin. "I'm not leaving."

"Me, neither," someone said. "I'm on Benny's side." Will stepped up beside Benny.

"And me," Carlos added, running to join them.

"Count me in," Nina said, next to Carlos. "And I'm tough."

Hank's grin faded. He looked at all the kids, then let go of Derrick's arm.

"Who cares?" he said. "You don't scare me." But he walked away very fast.

Benny grinned at his friends, then turned to Derrick. "You okay?"

Derrick rubbed his sore arm and wiped his face. "I think he almost broke my arm."

"I don't see any blood." Benny touched Derrick's arm gently. Derrick groaned.

"Benny!"

The sharp voice made both boys jump. Mrs. Rumpbill hurried up. She looked angry.

The kids around them hurried away.

"Benny, I just talked to Ms. Toymoto, and she didn't see you this morning. You skipped school! And now you're picking on Derrick?"

Benny's mouth dropped open.

"That'll mean suspension, young man!"

7

Deal

"*I didn't skip,*" *Benny said.* "*The secretary* said she didn't have time for me this morning. And you told me not to come back."

"It wasn't Benny who hurt me," Derrick told the teacher. "Benny came to help. And my arm hurts."

Mrs. Rumpbill sent Derrick to the school nurse. She looked at Benny, and Benny looked back.

"I'm not a troublemaker," Benny told her. "How come you always blame me?"

Mrs. Rumpbill pressed her lips together, but this time she didn't look angry. She looked a little bit guilty.

The bell rang, and the other students headed for the classrooms.

"Let me get the class settled," the teacher said. "Then I think we need to have a talk."

Benny wasn't sure he wanted another talk with Mrs. Rumpbill.

Mrs. Rumpbill instructed the students to open their books and told Nina she could take names of kids who broke rules. Then she and Benny walked back outside and sat on a bench beside the playground.

"Are you telling me that you haven't tried to cause trouble, Benny?"

"Only once, with the squirt bottle. I had this plan," he said. "I thought if I was impossible, you'd send me to Ms. Jackson's room." Benny stared at the ground, not wanting to meet his teacher's eye. "I mean, she has animals in her room and funny posters on the wall and lots of books to read. All my friends are in her class. But being bad is hard work."

"And the hamster?" Mrs. Rumpbill asked.

"I thought you'd like it. I was going to build a maze and do experiments," Benny explained. "Our room isn't any fun."

"I can't have animals or birds in my room, Benny," Mrs. Rumpbill said. "I have allergies to fur and feathers. I would sneeze so much I couldn't teach."

Benny thought that might not be so bad. "Fish don't have fur or feathers," he pointed out. "Snakes or turtles don't, either."

Mrs. Rumpbill looked thoughtful. "I know our room is bare, but I haven't had time to fix it up. I didn't know I was coming to this school until a day or two before the term started."

She didn't sound very happy about the memory.

Benny asked, "Did you want to come?"

Mrs. Rumpbill sighed. "I had my room all arranged at my old school, Benny. I had a big closet with much more room and corner windows that caught the breeze. I had good friends teaching in the same building."

Benny had never thought about a teacher having to give up her friends, too, or her favorite room. "That's rough," he said.

Mrs. Rumpbill smiled at him. "But sometimes we have to make new friends. And things work out better than we expected."

"That's what my grandpa said," Benny agreed. "He knows a lot."

"I'm sure he does. I'm sorry I was too quick to judge you. I think we should start over."

Mrs. Rumpbill held out her hand, and Benny shook it.

"Deal," he said.

They walked back to the classroom to-gether. When they walked into the room, all the kids stared.

"Benny and I have been talking," Mrs. Rumpbill told the class. "Benny has some good ideas to make our room more fun."

Benny looked at the teacher in surprise. He did?

"Tomorrow I'm bringing an aquarium to class; we're going to stock it with different kinds of fish. And we'll plan a terrarium, with turtles and frogs to watch."

"And snakes?" Benny asked hopefully.

"Turtles and frogs, first," Mrs. Rumpbill said.

"That sounds great," Will said. "Good thinking, Benny."

"Wow," Derrick agreed. "Nobody else in fourth grade has turtles and frogs."

"And fish can't climb out of their tank," Nina said happily.

Benny grinned.

"Right now, I've finally finished my seating plan," Mrs. Rumpbill told them. "We're going to change desks. Take out all your books."

The students emptied their desks. Nina whispered, "I hope you can sit by me, Benny."

Benny looked at her in surprise. Then he remembered the playground. She wasn't mad at him anymore. "You do?"

She gave him a big smile and fluttered her eyelashes. "Stacey explained why you've been picking on me, with the squirt bottle and the hamster and all."

"Explained what?" Benny asked.

"How a boy can like a special girl and not know how to show it, so he does silly things." Nina smiled at him again and shut her eyes. "You can kiss me if you want, Benny."

"Oh, gross," Benny said.

"What?" Nina opened her eyes wide.

"I said, oh, I have to go," Benny told her

quickly. He grabbed his books and hurried to the front of the room.

Mrs. Rumpbill told everyone where to sit. Thank goodness, Benny was up front, with Will and Stacey in the next row and Derrick behind him. Nina was on the side, two rows away.

But she waved at him.

Benny pretended not to see. He felt sure that Nina liking him would be even worse than Nina hating him.

Maybe he needed a Nina plan.